CARTOON NETWORK®

SCOOBY-DOO!™

MAD LIBS®

By Roger Price and Leonard Stern

PSS!
PRICE STERN SLOAN

MAD LIBS®

MAD LIBS® is a game for people who don't like games. It can be played by one, two, three, four, or forty.

■ RIDICULOUSLY SIMPLE DIRECTIONS

In this tablet you will find stories containing blank spaces where words are left out. One player, the **READER**, selects one of these stories. The **READER** does not tell anyone what the story is about. Instead he/she asks the other players, the **WRITERS**, to give him/her words. These words are used to fill in the blank spaces in the story.

■ TO PLAY

The **READER** asks each **WRITER** in turn to call out a word. This word will be an adjective or a noun or whatever the space calls for. He/she then writes the words in the blank spaces in the story. After all the spaces are filled in, the result is a **MAD LIBS®** game.

The **READER** then reads the completed **MAD LIBS®** game to the other players. They will hear that they have written a story that is fantastic, screamingly funny, shocking, silly, crazy, or just plain dumb—depending upon which words each **WRITER** called out.

In case you've forgotten what adjectives, adverbs, nouns, and verbs are, here is a quick review:

An **ADJECTIVE** describes something or somebody. *Lumpy*, *soft*, *ugly, messy*, and *short* are adjectives.

An **ADVERB** tells how something is done. It modifies a verb and usually ends in "ly." *Modestly, stupidly, greedily*, and *carefully* are adverbs.

A **NOUN** is the name of a person, place or thing. *Sidewalk, umbrella, bridle, bathtub* and *nose* are nouns.

A **VERB** is an action word. *Run, pitch, jump,* and *swim* are verbs. Put the verb in past tense if the directions say **PAST TENSE**. *Ran, pitched, jumped,* and *swam* are verbs in the past tense.

When we ask for a **GEOGRAPHICAL LOCATION**, we mean any sort of place: a country or city (Spain, Cleveland) or a room (bathroom, kitchen).

An **EXCLAMATION** or **SILLY WORD** is any sort of funny sound, gasp, grunt, or outcry. *Wow!, Ouch!, Whomp!, Ick!,* and *Gadzooks!* are exclamations and silly words.

When we ask for specific words like **A NUMBER, A COLOR, AN ANIMAL**, or **A PART OF THE BODY**, we mean a word that is one of those things.

When a **PLURAL** is asked for, be sure to pluralize the word. For example, *cat* pluralized is *cats.*

EXAMPLE:

(BEFORE)

" _____ !" he said

EXCLAMATION

_____ as he jumped into

ADVERB

his convertible _____ and

NOUN

drove off with his _____ wife.

ADJECTIVE

(AFTER)

" _____ *Ouch* _____ !" he said

EXCLAMATION

_____ *Stupidly* _____ as he jumped into his

ADVERB

convertible _____ *cat* _____ and drove

NOUN

off with his _____ *brave* _____ wife.

ADJECTIVE

MAD LIBS® is fun to play with friends, but you can also play it by yourself! To begin with, DO NOT look at the story on the page below. Fill in the blanks on this page with the words called for. Then, using the words you've selected, fill in the blank spaces in the story.

Now you've created your own hilarious MAD LIBS® game!

SCOOBY-DOO THE ACTOR, CHAPTER ONE

ADJECTIVE _____

NOUN _____

EXCLAMATION _____

FAMOUS PERSON _____

MOVIE STAR _____

ADJECTIVE _____

PERSON IN ROOM (MALE) _____

PART OF THE BODY _____

ADJECTIVE _____

ANIMAL _____

NOUN _____

"I have a/an _____ idea," Shaggy said.

ADJECTIVE

"Scooby-Doo can become a famous _____ in

NOUN

Hollywood, just like Lassie or Rin Tin Tin."

"_____!" said Freddy. "He is as good looking as

EXCLAMATION

_____ and as good an actor as

FAMOUS PERSON

_____." "Let's get him a tryout with the

MOVIE STAR

_____ movie director _____,"

ADJECTIVE   PERSON IN ROOM (MALE)

said Daphne. They put makeup all over Scooby-Doo's

_____ and got a/an _____

PART OF THE BODY   ADJECTIVE

_____ to play opposite him.

ANIMAL

When he saw the finished test, the director said, "Scooby-

Doo, you will star in my next _____."

NOUN

MAD LIBS® is fun to play with friends, but you can also play it by yourself! To begin with, DO NOT look at the story on the page below. Fill in the blanks on this page with the words called for. Then, using the words you've selected, fill in the blank spaces in the story.

Now you've created your own hilarious MAD LIBS® game!

SCOOBY-DOO THE ACTOR, CHAPTER TWO

NUMBER _____

ADJECTIVE _____

NOUN _____

ANIMAL _____

PLACE _____

NOUN _____

ADJECTIVE _____

NOUN _____

ADJECTIVE _____

NOUN _____

PLACE _____

NOUN _____

MAGAZINE _____

TELEVISION SHOW _____

MAD LIBS®
Scooby-Doo the Actor, Chapter Two

The movie director made a/an _____ -dollar
                                                 NUMBER

picture based on a/an _____ story called *Jack*,
                              ADJECTIVE

the _____ *Killer*. It was about a poor _____
          NOUN   ANIMAL

named Jack who journeyed to _____ to rescue a
                                  PLACE

beautiful _____ from a/an _____ giant.
             NOUN   ADJECTIVE

Scooby-Doo played the part of Jack, the _____ of the film.
                                        NOUN

The critics all said Scooby-Doo's performance was

_____ and he was certain to win a/an _____!
 ADJECTIVE   NOUN

Fans followed him all over_____ and begged him for
                             PLACE

his _____ . He was interviewed in _____
       NOUN   MAGAZINE

and appeared as a guest on _____.
                            TELEVISION SHOW

MAD LIBS® is fun to play with friends, but you can also play it by yourself! To begin with, DO NOT look at the story on the page below. Fill in the blanks on this page with the words called for. Then, using the words you've selected, fill in the blank spaces in the story.

Now you've created your own hilarious MAD LIBS® game!

SCOOBY-DOO THE ACTOR, CHAPTER THREE

ADJECTIVE _____

ADJECTIVE _____

PERSON'S NAME _____

ANOTHER PERSON'S NAME _____

FAMOUS PERSON _____

ANOTHER FAMOUS PERSON _____

ADJECTIVE _____

ADJECTIVE _____

EXCLAMATION _____

ADVERB _____

VERB _____

PLURAL NOUN _____

OCCUPATION _____

NOUN _____

There were some things about being a/an _____
ADJECTIVE

star that Scooby-Doo enjoyed. He liked eating in _____
ADJECTIVE

restaurants and appearing on television shows such as

"The _____ Show" and "The _____
PERSON'S NAME   ANOTHER PERSON'S NAME

Program." And people like _____ and
FAMOUS PERSON

_____ were always inviting him to _____
ANOTHER FAMOUS PERSON   ADJECTIVE

parties. But Scooby-Doo really wasn't very _____.
ADJECTIVE

"_____ !" he said _____ , "I never see
EXCLAMATION   ADVERB

Shaggy or Freddy or get to _____ at the beach or eat
VERB

_____ . I would rather be just a plain _____
PLURAL NOUN   OCCUPATION

than a movie star." So he packed his _____ and
NOUN

went home.

MAD LIBS® is fun to play with friends, but you can also play it by yourself! To begin with, DO NOT look at the story on the page below. Fill in the blanks on this page with the words called for. Then, using the words you've selected, fill in the blank spaces in the story.

Now you've created your own hilarious MAD LIBS® game!

SCOOBY-DOO'S BEACH PARTY

ADJECTIVE _____

MACHINE _____

VERB (PAST TENSE) _____

FAMOUS VACATION SPOT _____

ARTICLE OF CLOTHING (PLURAL) _____

PLURAL NOUN _____

BODY OF WATER _____

ADJECTIVE _____

PLURAL NOUN _____

OCCUPATION _____

PART OF THE BODY _____

ANIMAL _____

TYPE OF FOOD (PLURAL) _____

MAD LIBS®

Scooby-Doo's Beach Party

One day Freddy, Daphne, and Scooby-Doo decided to have a

_____ beach party. So they got some hot dogs and
ADJECTIVE

a portable _____. They then _____ to
MACHINE   VERB (PAST TENSE)

_____. Freddy and Daphne put on their bathing
FAMOUS VACATION SPOT

_____ and got out their surf _____.
ARTICLE OF CLOTHING (PLURAL)   PLURAL NOUN

Meanwhile, Scooby-Doo went down to the edge of the

_____ and began digging. To his surprise, in
BODY OF WATER

an hour, Scooby-Doo dug up a/an _____ chest
                                         ADJECTIVE

filled with _____.
                 PLURAL NOUN

When Freddy and Daphne came back, they said, "Wow,

Scooby-Doo, this must have belonged to a/an _____
                                                  OCCUPATION

who had a wooden _____ and went around with
                      PART OF THE BODY

a/an _____ on his shoulder." But all Scooby-Doo
          ANIMAL

was really hoping to find were _____!
                                    TYPE OF FOOD (PLURAL)

MAD LIBS® is fun to play with friends, but you can also play it by yourself! To begin with, DO NOT look at the story on the page below. Fill in the blanks on this page with the words called for. Then, using the words you've selected, fill in the blank spaces in the story.

Now you've created your own hilarious MAD LIBS® game!

A CLUE FOR SCOOBY-DOO, CHAPTER ONE

BODY OF WATER _____

ADJECTIVE _____

ARTICLE OF CLOTHING (PLURAL) _____

ADVERB _____

VERB (PAST TENSE) _____

ADJECTIVE _____

ADJECTIVE _____

NOUN _____

PERSON IN ROOM _____

NOUN _____

ADJECTIVE _____

VERB (PAST TENSE) _____

NOUN _____

ADVERB _____

MAD LIBS®
A Clue for Scooby-Doo, Chapter One

Scooby-Doo was surfing in the _____
                                          BODY OF WATER

when he bumped into a/an _____ ghost
                                      ADJECTIVE

dressed in deep-sea _____. "Ripes!"
                            ARTICLE OF CLOTHING (PLURAL)

Scooby yelped, as he _____ turned the
                                  ADVERB

surfboard and _____ back to the shore.
                        VERB (PAST TENSE)

The ghost followed Scooby on to the shore, but turned around

leaving _____ footprints in the sand.
                    ADJECTIVE

"That's _____," Velma said.
                  ADJECTIVE

The next day, Fred read the newspaper, "'Another

_____ vanishes' Fisherman _____ claims
      NOUN   PERSON IN ROOM

it's the work of the ghost of Captain Cutler. Months ago,

Cutler's _____ hit a _____ yacht sending it down
              NOUN   ADJECTIVE

to the ships' graveyard. Before the captain _____,
                                                        VERB (PAST TENSE)

he vowed to get his _____."
                            NOUN

"It sounds like a mystery to me!" Velma shouted _____.
                                                              ADVERB

MAD LIBS® is fun to play with friends, but you can also play it by yourself! To begin with, DO NOT look at the story on the page below. Fill in the blanks on this page with the words called for. Then, using the words you've selected, fill in the blank spaces in the story.

Now you've created your own hilarious MAD LIBS® game!

A CLUE FOR SCOOBY-DOO, CHAPTER TWO

PLURAL NOUN _____

PLURAL NOUN _____

ADJECTIVE _____

PLURAL NOUN _____

EXCLAMATION _____

VERB _____

PLURAL NOUN _____

NOUN _____

LIQUID _____

NOUN _____

NOUN _____

ADJECTIVE _____

ADJECTIVE _____

MAD LIBS®
A Clue for Scooby-Doo, Chapter Two

The gang rented some _____ and dove down

PLURAL NOUN

to investigate the graveyard of _____.

PLURAL NOUN

Scooby and Shaggy went inside the hold of a/an

_____ ship, where they found another clue—

ADJECTIVE

_____. They also ran into the ghost.

PLURAL NOUN

"_____!" Shaggy shouted. "_____

EXCLAMATION   VERB

for it, Scoob!" They found the rest of the gang in an

underground cavern filled with _____.

PLURAL NOUN

"We're setting a trap to catch the _____," Freddy said.

NOUN

Scooby was in charge of the net. When the ghost emerged from

the _____, Scooby pulled a/an _____ and

LIQUID   NOUN

the net fell on the ghost. "Captain Cutler!" Velma cried when

they removed his _____. "He's still alive!"

NOUN

"My _____ scheme has been ruined, thanks to

ADJECTIVE

you _____ kids!" he yelled, shaking his fists.

ADJECTIVE

"Scooby-Dooby Doo!" Scooby said.

MAD LIBS® is fun to play with friends, but you can also play it by yourself! To begin with, DO NOT look at the story on the page below. Fill in the blanks on this page with the words called for. Then, using the words you've selected, fill in the blank spaces in the story.

Now you've created your own hilarious MAD LIBS® game!

SCOOBY-DOO CATCHES A GHOST

VERB ENDING IN "ING" _____

ADJECTIVE _____

PLURAL NOUN _____

PLURAL NOUN _____

NOUN _____

EXCLAMATION _____

VERB _____

VERB _____

NOUN _____

EXCLAMATION _____

ADJECTIVE _____

NOUN _____

MAD LIBS®

Scooby-Doo Catches a Ghost

One night, Scooby and Shaggy were _____
                                    VERB ENDING IN "ING"

by a/an _____ cemetery. "Do you think there are
         ADJECTIVE

any ghosts of dead _____ in there?" Shaggy
                        PLURAL NOUN

asked. "Ro-Ray," Scooby said. He knew ghosts were just

imaginary _____.
           PLURAL NOUN

Suddenly, a big white_____ jumped out at them.
                          NOUN

"_____!" said Scooby, as he and Shaggy began to
   EXCLAMATION

_____with fright. They both tried to
        VERB

out-_____ the figure, but they tripped over a
       VERB

_____ and crashed into the ghost.
     NOUN

"_____!" said the ghost.
   EXCLAMATION

"Hey," Shaggy said. "That ghost sounds _____!"
                                          ADJECTIVE

Sure enough, it turned out to be Freddy, who was trying to

scare them by pretending to be a/an _____.
                                        NOUN

MAD LIBS® is fun to play with friends, but you can also play it by yourself! To begin with, DO NOT look at the story on the page below. Fill in the blanks on this page with the words called for. Then, using the words you've selected, fill in the blank spaces in the story.

Now you've created your own hilarious MAD LIBS® game!

SCOOBY-DOO AND THE GOLD MINE

NOUN _____

COLOR _____

METAL _____

ADJECTIVE _____

NOUN _____

VEHICLE _____

SAME METAL _____

ADJECTIVE _____

PLURAL NOUN _____

ADJECTIVE _____

PLURAL NOUN _____

SAME METAL _____

ADJECTIVE _____

MAD LIBS®
Scooby-Doo and the Gold Mine

One day, Scooby and Shaggy were digging a/an _____
NOUN

near a cave, when Shaggy found a hunk of _____ rock.
COLOR

"Whoa, that might be real _____ ," he said. So they
METAL

decided to explore the _____ cave. Scooby wondered
ADJECTIVE

if it might be a/an _____ mine.
NOUN

"Look, there is a little _____ that they used to
VEHICLE

bring the _____ out of the mine." They went deeper
SAME METAL

into the _____ cave. It was filled with spider
ADJECTIVE

_____ and _____ bats. They found
PLURAL NOUN   ADJECTIVE

a pile of rusty _____ , but no _____
PLURAL NOUN   SAME METAL

They realized it wasn't an empty mine, just a/an _____ cave.
ADJECTIVE

MAD LIBS® is fun to play with friends, but you can also play it by yourself! To begin with, DO NOT look at the story on the page below. Fill in the blanks on this page with the words called for. Then, using the words you've selected, fill in the blank spaces in the story.

Now you've created your own hilarious MAD LIBS® game!

SCOOBY-DOO THE GUARD DOG, CHAPTER ONE

NOUN _____

ANIMAL _____

ADJECTIVE _____

ANIMAL _____

ADVERB _____

MUSICAL INSTRUMENT _____

ADJECTIVE _____

ADJECTIVE _____

ADVERB _____

VERB _____

ADJECTIVE _____

MAD LIBS
Scooby-Doo the Guard Dog, Chapter One

Freddy saw a/an _____ in the paper that
                        NOUN

said "Wanted: A well trained _____ to guard
                                    ANIMAL

a/an _____ pudding factory."
            ADJECTIVE

"Scooby-Dooby-Doo," Scooby-Doo said.

"You could be a guard _____," Freddy
                                ANIMAL

agreed _____. "I'll get you a little _____
            ADVERB   MUSICAL INSTRUMENT

you can blow if anyone comes around."

"Wait a second," Shaggy said. "He'll have to learn to be

_____ and attack _____ people."
        ADJECTIVE   ADJECTIVE

"Rattack?" Scooby-Doo said _____. "Ruh-Ro!"
                                    ADVERB

"Well, if you want the job, you'll have to _____
                                                    VERB

to a school and learn to be _____," Shaggy said.
                                    ADJECTIVE

MAD LIBS® is fun to play with friends, but you can also play it by yourself! To begin with, DO NOT look at the story on the page below. Fill in the blanks on this page with the words called for. Then, using the words you've selected, fill in the blank spaces in the story.

Now you've created your own hilarious MAD LIBS® game!

SCOOBY-DOO THE GUARD DOG,
CHAPTER TWO

PERSON'S LAST NAME _____

PERSON IN ROOM (FEMALE) _____

ANIMAL _____

ADJECTIVE _____

VERB _____

VERB _____

VERB _____

ADJECTIVE _____

ADJECTIVE _____

NOUN _____

VERB _____

NOUN _____

ADJECTIVE _____

MAD LIBS
Scooby-Doo the Guard Dog, Chapter Two

The head of the _____ Obedience
PERSON'S LAST NAME

School was _____ . She said she would
PERSON IN ROOM (FEMALE)

teach Scooby-Doo to be a real guard _____ .
ANIMAL

"You must learn to bite and use Judo and Karate."

"He's a/an _____ dog," Shaggy said. "He would
ADJECTIVE

rather _____ than _____ ."
VERB   VERB

Scooby-Doo never learned to _____ , but he
VERB

learned to make _____ faces and utter
ADJECTIVE

_____ noises, and they gave him the chance to
ADJECTIVE

guard the _____ factory.
NOUN

"If any burglars come around," the owners said, "you

_____ and push this _____ , which
VERB   NOUN

sets off a/an _____ alarm."
ADJECTIVE

MAD LIBS® is fun to play with friends, but you can also play it by yourself! To begin with, DO NOT look at the story on the page below. Fill in the blanks on this page with the words called for. Then, using the words you've selected, fill in the blank spaces in the story.

Now you've created your own hilarious MAD LIBS® game!

SCOOBY-DOO THE GUARD DOG, CHAPTER THREE

NOUN _____

ADJECTIVE _____

ADJECTIVE _____

FUNNY NOISE _____

PART OF THE BODY (PLURAL) _____

VERB (PAST TENSE) _____

FUNNY NOISE _____

EXCLAMATION _____

VERB _____

PLURAL NOUN _____

PLURAL NOUN _____

PLURAL NOUN _____

The pudding factory Scooby-Doo was guarding had a

big iron _____ at the entrance.
　　　　　　　NOUN

This is _____ , Scooby-Doo thought. Just then
　　　　　ADJECTIVE

he heard a/an _____ sound. It went
　　　　　　　　　　　ADJECTIVE

" _____ ." Instantly, Scooby-Doo's
　　　　FUNNY NOISE

_____ stood up as he _____.
PART OF THE BODY (PLURAL)　　　　　　　　VERB (PAST TENSE)

Sure enough, he heard " _____."
　　　　　　　　　　　　FUNNY NOISE

" _____!" Scooby-Doo said, and he began to
　　　EXCLAMATION

_____ out of there. But just then he saw three big,
VERB

scary _____ carrying _____ and
　　　PLURAL NOUN　　　　　　　　　PLURAL NOUN

wearing black _____ on their faces.
　　　　　　　PLURAL NOUN

MAD LIBS® is fun to play with friends, but you can also play it by yourself! To begin with, DO NOT look at the story on the page below. Fill in the blanks on this page with the words called for. Then, using the words you've selected, fill in the blank spaces in the story.

Now you've created your own hilarious MAD LIBS® game!

SCOOBY-DOO THE GUARD DOG, CHAPTER FOUR

EXCLAMATION _____

ADJECTIVE _____

PLACE _____

COLOR _____

NOUN _____

NOUN _____

FLAVOR _____

ADVERB _____

PLURAL NOUN _____

EXCLAMATION _____

PLURAL NOUN _____

ADJECTIVE _____

NOUN _____

"_____ !" Scooby-Doo said when he saw the
　　　EXCLAMATION

_____ burglars. So he ran to _____ and
　　ADJECTIVE　　　　　　　　　　　　　　　　　　　　PLACE

pushed a big _____ button. However, it wasn't
　　　　　　　　　COLOR

the alarm _____. Scooby-Doo pushed a/an
　　　　　　　　NOUN

_____ that opened a big vat of _____ pudding.
　NOUN　　　　　　　　　　　　　　　　　　　FLAVOR

The pudding _____ slid down into the street and
　　　　　　　　　ADVERB

landed right on the evil _____ who were trying
　　　　　　　　　　　　　PLURAL NOUN

to rob the factory.

"_____ !" they said. "We're stuck!"
　　EXCLAMATION

Then Scooby-Doo pushed the button, and the police came

with their _____ screaming. They arrested all of
　　　　　　PLURAL NOUN

the _____ burglars and told Scooby-Doo he was
　　　ADJECTIVE

a real _____.
　　　　NOUN

MAD LIBS® is fun to play with friends, but you can also play it by yourself! To begin with, DO NOT look at the story on the page below. Fill in the blanks on this page with the words called for. Then, using the words you've selected, fill in the blank spaces in the story.

Now you've created your own hilarious MAD LIBS® game!

SCOOBY-DOO, OPERA SINGER, CHAPTER ONE

ADJECTIVE _____

FAMOUS PERSON_____

ADJECTIVE_____

ANIMAL _____

VERB _____

VERB ENDING IN "ING"_____

NOUN _____

PART OF THE BODY _____

VERB (PAST TENSE)_____

EXCLAMATION_____

VERB_____

One day, Velma decided that Scooby-Doo had such a/an

_____ voice that he should be an opera singer.
     ADJECTIVE

"He could be another _____," Velma said.
                       FAMOUS PERSON

Shaggy said, "If you ask me, when he sings, he sounds

like a/an _____ _____."
          ADJECTIVE   ANIMAL

But the owner of the opera house didn't have time to

hear Scooby _____.
               VERB

"A phantom is _____ all over my opera!" he
              VERB ENDING IN "ING"

said. Just then, a figure wearing a/an _____, and a mask
                           NOUN

over his _____ _____ across the stage!
       PART OF THE BODY   VERB (PAST TENSE)

"_____!" Shaggy said. "There really is a
       EXCLAMATION

phantom! Let's _____!"
              VERB

MAD LIBS® is fun to play with friends, but you can also play it by yourself! To begin with, DO NOT look at the story on the page below. Fill in the blanks on this page with the words called for. Then, using the words you've selected, fill in the blank spaces in the story.

Now you've created your own hilarious MAD LIBS® game!

SCOOBY-DOO, OPERA SINGER, CHAPTER TWO

PLURAL NOUN _____

ADJECTIVE _____

ADVERB _____

VERB _____

ADVERB _____

ADJECTIVE _____

VERB _____

ADJECTIVE _____

ADJECTIVE _____

VERB _____

PLURAL NOUN _____

VERB (PAST TENSE) _____

Scooby-Doo, Opera Singer,
Chapter Two

Shaggy and Scooby hid from the phantom in a closet full of

_____. "That's one _____ phantom!"
　　　　PLURAL NOUN　　　　　　　　　　　　　ADJECTIVE

Shaggy said _____. "I hope Velma's all right.
　　　　　　　　　　ADVERB

Maybe we should _____ out and look for her."
　　　　　　　　　　　　　VERB

Shaggy and Scooby looked around _____.
　　　　　　　　　　　　　　　　　　　　　　　ADVERB

The coast was _____, so they began to _____
　　　　　　　　ADJECTIVE　　　　　　　　　　　　　VERB

down a long, _____ hallway. Just then, they
　　　　　　　ADJECTIVE

heard a/an _____ scream. Their first instinct
　　　　　　　　ADJECTIVE

was to _____, but they knew Velma needed
　　　　　VERB

_____, so they _____ toward the noise.
　PLURAL NOUN　　　　　　　VERB (PAST TENSE)

MAD LIBS® is fun to play with friends, but you can also play it by yourself! To begin with, DO NOT look at the story on the page below. Fill in the blanks on this page with the words called for. Then, using the words you've selected, fill in the blank spaces in the story.

Now you've created your own hilarious MAD LIBS® game!

SCOOBY-DOO, OPERA SINGER, CHAPTER THREE

ADJECTIVE _____

PART OF THE BODY _____

VERB ENDING IN "ING" _____

PART OF THE BODY _____

NOUN _____

VERB ENDING IN "ING" _____

PART OF THE BODY (PLURAL) _____

VERB _____

NOUN _____

PLURAL NOUN _____

Scooby-Doo, Opera Singer
Chapter Three

Scooby came to a/an _____ halt when he
ADJECTIVE

and Shaggy reached the stage. From there, they could see the

phantom. He had his _____ wrapped around
PART OF THE BODY

Velma and was _____ on the balcony.
VERB ENDING IN "ING"

Scooby had to try to stop him! From the center of the

stage, he opened his _____ and began to sing
PART OF THE BODY

He sounded like a/an _____ _____
NOUN   VERB ENDING IN "ING"

and the phantom had to cover his ears with his

_____ to block out the sound.
PART OF THE BODY (PLURAL)

Velma was able to escape, but before the phantom could

_____, Scooby's singing caused a/an _____ that
VERB   NOUN

hung from the ceiling to crash down and trap him.

"Well Scooby," Shaggy said after the _____
PLURAL NOUN

came and arrested the phantom, "no one can say you didn't

bring the house down as an opera singer!"

MAD LIBS® is fun to play with friends, but you can also play it by yourself! To begin with, DO NOT look at the story on the page below. Fill in the blanks on this page with the words called for. Then, using the words you've selected, fill in the blank spaces in the story.

Now you've created your own hilarious MAD LIBS® game!

SCOOBY-DOO ENTERS A SHOW

NOUN _____

ANIMAL _____

ADVERB _____

COLOR _____

ADJECTIVE _____

ADJECTIVE _____

SOMEONE IN ROOM _____

SAME ANIMAL _____

BUILDING _____

VERB _____

ADJECTIVE _____

NOUN _____

Shaggy pointed to a/an _____ in the newspaper.
NOUN

"There is going to be a big _____ show," he said
ANIMAL

_____ . "We should enter Scooby-Doo."
ADVERB

Scooby-Doo thought he could win a/an _____
COLOR

ribbon. Everyone told him that for a/an _____
ADJECTIVE

Dane, he was really _____.
ADJECTIVE

The next day the gang all went to the _____
SOMEONE IN ROOM

Memorial Stadium for the _____ show. The judges
SAME ANIMAL

watched Scooby-Doo walk around the _____ and
BUILDING

they said, "_____," and Scooby-Doo did.
VERB

"That is really a/an _____ dog," the head judge
ADJECTIVE

said. And so they awarded Scooby-Doo the title of "Best

_____ in the Show."
NOUN

MAD LIBS® is fun to play with friends, but you can also play it by yourself! To begin with, DO NOT look at the story on the page below. Fill in the blanks on this page with the words called for. Then, using the words you've selected, fill in the blank spaces in the story.

Now you've created your own hilarious MAD LIBS® game!

SCOOBY-DOO AT THE SKI RESORT

NOUN_____

NUMBER _____

PLURAL NOUN_____

ADJECTIVE_____

ANIMAL _____

ADJECTIVE _____

EXCLAMATION _____

SOMETHING TO DRINK _____

PLURAL NOUN_____

PART OF THE BODY (PLURAL) _____

NUMBER _____

ADJECTIVE_____

ADJECTIVE_____

SOMETHING TO DRINK _____

NOUN _____

PLURAL NOUN_____

MAD LIBS®
Scooby-Doo at the Ski Resort

Scooby-Doo went with Velma and Shaggy to a ski lodge. When

they got there, the _____ was _____ feet
NOUN · NUMBER

deep. The manager said that two _____
PLURAL NOUN

were lost in the _____ snow.
ADJECTIVE

"We usually have a St. Bernard _____ to
ANIMAL

rescue people. But he is _____."
ADJECTIVE

"_____!" Velma said. "Scooby-Doo
EXCLAMATION

will be glad to help you." So they put a quart of

_____ around Scooby-Doo's neck and
SOMETHING TO DRINK

put _____ on his _____.
PLURAL NOUN · PART OF THE BODY (PLURAL)

Then Scooby-Doo headed up the mountain. About _____
NUMBER

miles away he found the _____ skiers. They
ADJECTIVE

were almost frozen _____. Scooby-Doo gave
ADJECTIVE

them some hot _____ and led them back
SOMETHING TO DRINK

to the _____.
NOUN

"You're a hero," Shaggy exclaimed. "You've saved

their _____!"
PLURAL NOUN

MAD LIBS® is fun to play with friends, but you can also play it by yourself! To begin with, DO NOT look at the story on the page below. Fill in the blanks on this page with the words called for. Then, using the words you've selected, fill in the blank spaces in the story.

Now you've created your own hilarious MAD LIBS® game!

SPOOKY SPACE ALIEN, CHAPTER ONE

LIQUID _____

PLACE _____

ADJECTIVE _____

NOUN _____

PLURAL NOUN _____

ADJECTIVE _____

PLACE _____

NOUN _____

ADJECTIVE _____

NOUN _____

ADJECTIVE _____

ADJECTIVE _____

NOUN _____

VERB _____

Spooky Space Alien,
Chapter One

The Mystery Machine had run out of _____

_____
LIQUID

in the middle of _____. Velma spotted a/an

_____
PLACE

_____ farmhouse, and the gang decided to

_____
ADJECTIVE

go for help. But the farmer who answered the door said, "You

should get off my _____ before the _____

_____ _____
NOUN PLURAL NOUN

get you. They've come in a/an _____ craft from

_____
ADJECTIVE

_____ and they've invaded my _____!"

_____ _____
PLACE NOUN

"Sounds _____, let's get out of here,"

_____
ADJECTIVE

Shaggy exclaimed.

"No way," said Velma. "We have a/an _____ to solve!"

_____
NOUN

Parking the Mystery Machine outside a/an _____

_____
ADJECTIVE

airfield, they soon spotted the _____ glowing

_____
ADJECTIVE

ghost craft.

"Look, it landed behind that _____," Fred

_____
NOUN

said. "Let's _____!"

_____
VERB

MAD LIBS® is fun to play with friends, but you can also play it by yourself! To begin with, DO NOT look at the story on the page below. Fill in the blanks on this page with the words called for. Then, using the words you've selected, fill in the blank spaces in the story.

Now you've created your own hilarious MAD LIBS® game!

SPOOKY SPACE ALIEN, CHAPTER TWO

TYPE OF CONTAINER _____

ADJECTIVE _____

TYPE OF FOOD_____

ANOTHER FOOD _____

ADJECTIVE_____

NOUN _____

EXCLAMATION_____

VERB _____

NOUN _____

ARTICLE OF CLOTHING_____

PERSON IN ROOM (MALE) _____

ADJECTIVE _____

NOUN _____

PLACE _____

ADVERB _____

MAD LIBS
Spooky Space Alien, Chapter Two

Searching for the space alien, Scooby and Shaggy found a/an

_____ full of food. While Scooby had a/an
TYPE OF CONTAINER

_____ snack of _____ and _____,
ADJECTIVE   TYPE OF FOOD   ANOTHER FOOD

Shaggy heard a/an _____ giggle outside the kitchen.
ADJECTIVE

Outside, Shaggy and Scooby ran into a glowing

_____ inside a space suit.
NOUN

"_____ !" cried Shaggy. "_____ for it!"
EXCLAMATION   VERB

They ran into the rest of the gang along with the farmer.

Meanwhile, the alien ran inside a/an _____ with
NOUN

a wind tunnel and was trapped. Scooby hit the switch, and

the alien's _____ blew off.
ARTICLE OF CLOTHING

"That's my neighbor, _____!" the farmer said.
PERSON IN ROOM (MALE)

"He used _____ effects to scare people off
ADJECTIVE

your _____," Daphne informed him.
NOUN

"Right," Scooby agreed.

"But now he'll be going to _____ , thanks to
PLACE

you kids and your dog," the farmer said _____.
ADVERB

MAD LIBS® is fun to play with friends, but you can also play it by yourself! To begin with, DO NOT look at the story on the page below. Fill in the blanks on this page with the words called for. Then, using the words you've selected, fill in the blank spaces in the story.

Now you've created your own hilarious MAD LIBS® game!

SCOOBY-DOO AND THE CREEPY CARNIVAL, CHAPTER ONE

VERB (PAST TENSE) _____

ADJECTIVE _____

ADJECTIVE _____

PERSON IN ROOM (MALE) _____

PROFESSION _____

ADJECTIVE _____

ADVERB _____

PLURAL NOUN _____

EXCLAMATION _____

TYPE OF CONTAINER _____

ADVERB _____

VERB (PAST TENSE) _____

COLOR _____

ANIMAL _____

ADVERB _____

The Scooby gang had _____ to a/an
VERB (PAST TENSE)

_____ amusement park. They were searching for
ADJECTIVE

the _____ jeweler _____, who had
ADJECTIVE PERSON IN ROOM (MALE)

disappeared. Colonel Tom, the carnival's _____,
PROFESSION

explained, "I had to shut the place down. People think it's

_____."
ADJECTIVE

_____, Velma looked on the ground, where
ADVERB

she saw a trail of _____. "_____!"
PLURAL NOUN EXCLAMATION

she exclaimed. "It's a clue!"

"The jeweler was carrying a/an _____ full of
TYPE OF CONTAINER

rubies," Fred said _____. "He must have
ADVERB

_____this way."
VERB (PAST TENSE)

Suddenly, Scooby and Shaggy were surprised by a/an

_____-bearded pirate with a/an _____ on his
COLOR ANIMAL

shoulder. They screamed and _____ ran away.
ADVERB

MAD LIBS® is fun to play with friends, but you can also play it by yourself! To begin with, DO NOT look at the story on the page below. Fill in the blanks on this page with the words called for. Then, using the words you've selected, fill in the blank spaces in the story.

Now you've created your own hilarious MAD LIBS® game!

SCOOBY-DOO AND THE CREEPY CARNIVAL, CHAPTER TWO

PLURAL NOUN _____

ADJECTIVE _____

ADJECTIVE _____

EXCLAMATION _____

NUMBER _____

VERB ENDING IN "ING" _____

NOUN _____

VERB (PAST TENSE) _____

PLURAL NOUN _____

ARTICLE OF CLOTHING _____

PLURAL NOUN _____

ADVERB _____

Outside the "House of _____" the
<small>PLURAL NOUN</small>

gang spotted some more rubies.

"There's a/an _____ trail of them!"
<small>ADJECTIVE</small>

They followed the trail down a/an _____
<small>ADJECTIVE</small>

staircase. At the bottom, they found the missing jeweler.

"_____!" he cried. "I've been trapped in here
<small>EXCLAMATION</small>

for _____ days!"
<small>NUMBER</small>

Meanwhile, the pirate was still _____
<small>VERB ENDING IN "ING"</small>

after Shaggy and Scooby. To escape, they jumped on a ride

that was shaped like a/an _____.
<small>NOUN</small>

When Shaggy pulled the on switch, the pirate _____
<small>VERB (PAST TENSE)</small>

into the air, landing in a pile of _____.
<small>PLURAL NOUN</small>

When his _____ was removed, the villain turned
<small>ARTICLE OF CLOTHING</small>

out to be Colonel Tom, the owner of the carnival. "If it

hadn't been for you kids and that dog, I could have stolen a

fortune in _____," he said _____!
<small>PLURAL NOUN</small>   <small>ADVERB</small>

This book is published by

PSS!
PRICE STERN SLOAN

**whose other splendid titles include
such literary classics as**

The Original #1 Mad Libs®
Son of Mad Libs®
Sooper Dooper Mad Libs®
Monster Mad Libs®
Goofy Mad Libs®
Off-the-Wall Mad Libs®
Vacation Fun Mad Libs®
Camp Daze Mad Libs®
Christmas Fun Mad Libs®
Mad Libs® from Outer Space
Grab Bag Mad Libs®
Kid Libs®
Dinosaur Mad Libs®
Slam Dunk Mad Libs®
Night of the Living Mad Libs®
Upside-Down Mad Libs®
Mad Libs® 40th Anniversary Deluxe Edition
Mad Mad Mad Mad Mad Libs®
Mad Libs® on the Road
Mad Libs® for President
Mad Libs® in Love

and many, many more!

Mad Libs ® are available wherever books are sold.